IRON JOHN

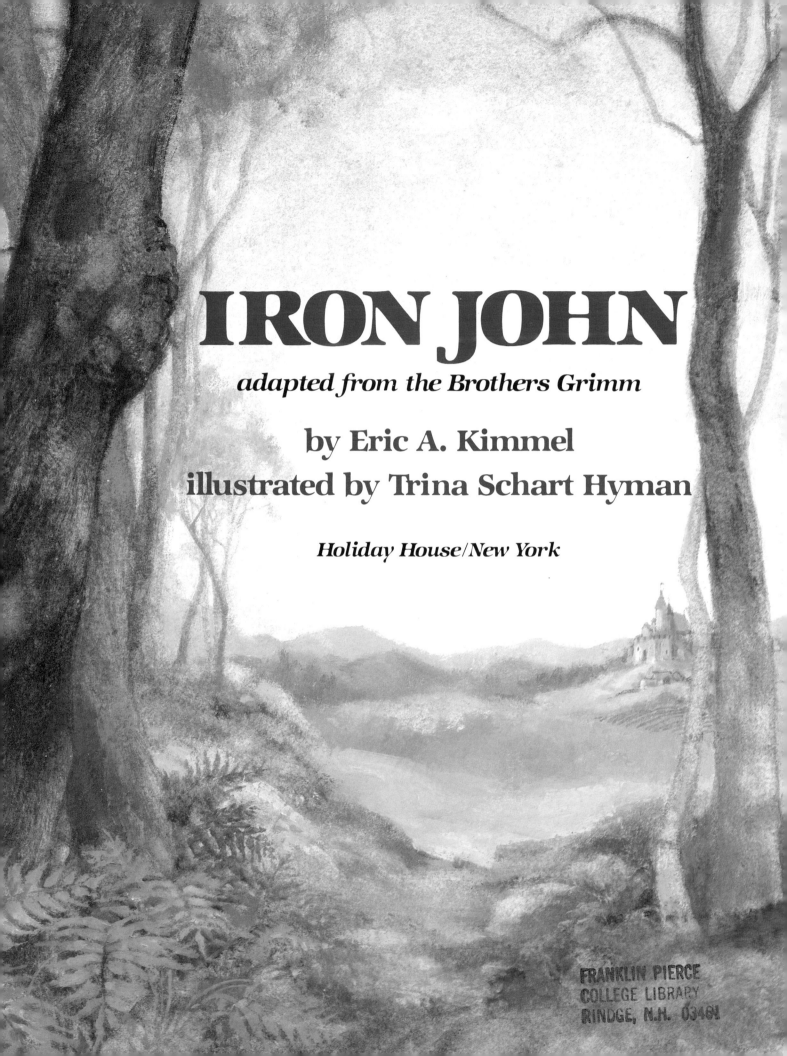

IRON JOHN

adapted from the Brothers Grimm

by Eric A. Kimmel

illustrated by Trina Schart Hyman

Holiday House/New York

For Doris
E.A.K.

To the memory of
David Rogers and Chuck Mikolaycak
T.S.H.

Text copyright © 1994 by Eric A. Kimmel
Illustrations copyright © 1994 by Trina Schart Hyman
All rights reserved
Printed in the United States of America
Library of Congress Cataloging-in-Publication Data
Kimmel, Eric A.
Iron John : adapted from the Brothers Grimm / by Eric A.
Kimmel ; illustrated by Trina Schart Hyman. — 1st ed.
        p.   cm.
Summary: With help of Iron John, the wild man of the forest
who is under a curse, a young prince makes his way in the world
and finds his true love.
ISBN 0-8234-1073-0
[1. Fairy tales.   2. Folklore—Germany.]   I. Grimm, Jacob,
1785–1863.   II. Grimm, Wilhelm, 1786–1859.   III. Hyman, Trina
Schart, ill.   IV. Eisenhans.   V. Title.
PZ8.K527Ir   1994   93-7534   CIP   AC
                398.21—dc20
                     [E]
         ISBN 0-8234-1248-2 (pbk.)

A king once lived who took great pride in his menagerie of beasts. He owned creatures of every description, from quivering shrews to trumpeting elephants. But the jewel of his collection was a wild man called Iron John, after the matted gray hair that covered his body from head to foot. Iron John was fiercer than a tiger. The bars of his cage were thicker than a man's wrist. No creature in the whole menagerie was as feared as Iron John.

One day, while the king was out riding, his youngest son Walter entered the menagerie park to play with his golden ball. A gust of wind caught it and carried it into Iron John's cage. Walter approached the cage fearfully and said to the wild man, "Iron John, please give me back my ball."

The wild man answered, "Will you free me if I do?"

"I would if I possessed the key," Walter stammered. "My father has hidden it, I know not where."

"Go to your mother's bedroom," said Iron John. "The key is beneath her pillow."

Walter hastened to his mother's bedroom. He lifted her pillow. There lay the key. Walter took it back and fitted it to the lock on Iron John's cage. The door sprang open. Iron John leaped out and climbed the menagerie wall. He paused at the top to throw down the golden ball. Walter cried to him, "Iron John, take me with you. When my father finds you gone, he will punish me for sure."

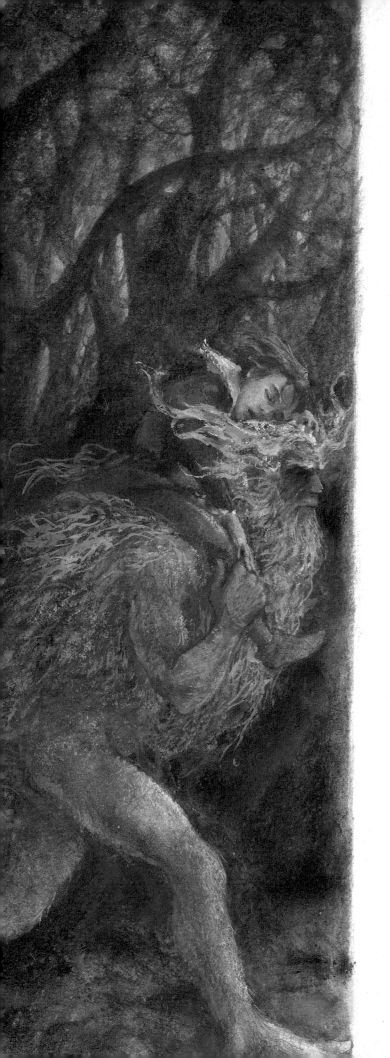

"Come with me then, but know you will see your home no more," Iron John said. The wild man leaped down and caught the lad in his arms. He cleared the wall with a single bound and vanished into the forest.

Iron John ran for a day and a night, following secret trails until he came to a hidden spring. He set Walter down.

"The forest is my home," the wild man told the boy. "Here I am king. Nothing can harm you, save by my word. I roam these woods by day and return by night. While I am gone, you must watch over my spring. See that nothing falls into it."

Walter guarded the spring faithfully. Through summer's heat and winter's cold, he watched to see that nothing fouled its waters. Years passed. Walter grew to manhood. His hair grew thick and long. He dressed in the skins of wild animals. Iron John taught him the ways of the forest. Walter loved the wild man as if he were his own father.

One day, as Walter sat beside the spring combing out his long, tangled locks, a hair dropped from the comb into the water. Walter plucked it out. The hair, to his surprise, had turned to purest gold.

When Iron John returned that evening, he said to Walter, "Something has fallen into my spring."

"That cannot be. I guarded it faithfully," Walter replied. But Iron John said, "Tell me the truth. It was a hair, was it not?"

Walter admitted it was.

"No harm was done," Iron John said. "The spring will recover. But you must be doubly careful in the future."

A few days later, on a warm afternoon, Walter lay peeling an apple beside the spring. The knife slipped and cut his finger. Without thinking, Walter plunged it into the spring. When he drew it out, his entire finger from the knuckle down had turned to gold. Fearing Iron John's wrath, Walter wrapped his finger in leaves.

That night, when Iron John returned, he asked Walter, "What happened to your finger?"

"I cut myself," Walter replied.

Iron John unwrapped the leafy bandage. The shimmer of gold shined through. "What is done cannot be undone," Iron John said. "The spring has been seriously damaged. It may recover, but you must guard it more carefully now than ever before. Were anything else to touch its waters, the precious spring would lose its power. You and I would have to part."

Walter vowed to do better.

Some time after that, on a sweltering summer day, as Walter sat in the cool shade beside the spring, he noticed something moving in its watery blue depths. Was it a fish? Walter had never seen a fish or any other living thing in the spring before. He leaned over for a closer look. His long hair tumbled forward and fell into the spring. Walter pulled it out, but it was too late. The locks of his hair had become a shining mass of gold.

Terrified of Iron John's wrath, Walter tied up his hair in a cloth. When Iron John returned that evening and asked why he had tied a cloth around his hair, Walter replied, "The gnats were biting. I covered my hair so they wouldn't sting me."

"Your hair and not your face?" Iron John asked. He untied the cloth. Walter's golden hair fell around his shoulders, shimmering forth like sunbeams.

"The spring is lost," Iron John said. "But do not grieve. It was made for this purpose. Now I must leave you. When you wake in the morning, tie up your hair, smear yourself with mud, and follow the rising sun to the edge of the forest. You will meet a king. Tell him you wish to serve him. If people ask your name, say it is 'Walter-in-the-Mud.' " He gave Walter a golden horn and some rough clothes. "If you ever need me, come to the spring and blow this horn three times." Then the wild man slipped away into the forest shadows. Walter saw him no more.

Walter arose the next morning. He tied up his hair and covered himself with mud from the spring. Then he followed the rising sun to the edge of the forest, where he saw a castle in the distance. He began walking toward it. Along the way he met a king on horseback. Three haughty princesses rode beside him.

The king greeted Walter. "Good day to you, young fellow."

"Good day to you, Your Majesty," Walter replied. "Might you have need of a servant? I seek a position."

"These three princesses, my daughters, have need of a serving man. But you will have to bathe. They could not abide one so filthy."

"Or so smelly," one of the princesses added, holding a perfumed handkerchief to her nose. "Why are you covered with mud? Why do you wear that cloth wrapped around your head?"

"I have sores on my skin and on my scalp," Walter explained. "The mud soothes them."

The princesses turned away in disgust. The king said, "Then you cannot stay in the palace. The garden girl needs a helper. Elsa is a good-hearted wench. She will not mind your sores. I daresay she is as dirty as you are."

The king sent Walter to work in the gardens. When Elsa, the garden girl, asked his name, he answered, "Walter-in-the-Mud." The name suited him, for if he was muddy before, within a few days he was black with dirt. Elsa became his friend. She never mocked him or complained about his smell. She was as dirty as he was.

One afternoon Elsa came to the garden with exciting news. "The king is holding a masked ball. The princesses say we may watch from the terrace if we make their bouquets. Oh, Walter, I have never seen a masked ball. How grand it will be!"

Walter helped Elsa make three bouquets of red, white, and yellow roses to bring to the princesses. Along the way he gathered a nosegay of wildflowers, which he hid in his shirt.

Walter returned to the forest that evening. He washed himself in the hidden spring and blew the golden horn three times. When Iron John appeared, Walter said to him, "Iron John, help me. I want to go to the king's ball. I need clothes to wear and a horse to ride."

"I will provide what you require," Iron John said. He disappeared behind the trees and returned a little while later leading a shining steed, bridled and saddled with purest gold. From the saddle hung a golden suit of clothes that glittered like the sun. Walter dressed quickly. Slipping on a golden mask and a pair of golden gloves, he galloped away.

Who was this shining stranger, so splendidly dressed? The princesses could not tell, though he danced with each in turn. They waited impatiently for midnight, when the dancers unmasked.

Before the clock struck twelve, the stranger slipped out the door. He leaped to his horse and rode away, pausing only long enough to pluck a nosegay of wildflowers from his shirt and toss it onto the terrace where Elsa the garden girl sat watching the ball through the window. She caught it in her lap. The crowd of princes and princesses nearly trampled her in their rush to follow the golden stranger. But he had disappeared into the night.

Elsa couldn't wait to tell Walter about the ball. "You should have come. It was splendid! The handsomest prince appeared, dressed all in gold. The princesses have fallen in love with him, but no one knows who he is or where he comes from. He threw a nosegay before he left, and I caught it! I am the luckiest of all." She continued, "And did you hear? There is to be a tournament. The bravest knights in the land will come. The princesses say we may watch from beneath the stands, if we keep out of sight. Oh, Walter, it will be so grand!"

The next morning Walter went to the forest to bathe in the spring. He blew his horn three times, and when Iron John appeared, Walter said to him, "The king is holding a tournament. I must have a suit of jousting armor and a charger to ride."

"I will provide what you require," Iron John answered. He disappeared into the forest and returned leading a mighty steed covered with a cloth-of-gold and carrying a lance and a gilded suit of jousting armor. Walter donned the armor with Iron John's help, then mounted to the saddle and rode away.

Who was this golden knight who charged into the lists and unhorsed one champion after another until no challenger remained? The princesses, giddy with excitement, placed the victor's garland on his lance, then waited expectantly for him to lay it at the feet of the maiden who would be the tournament's Queen of Love and Beauty. Each hoped he would choose her. To their chagrin the golden knight rode behind the stands and laid the garland at the bare and muddy feet of Elsa the garden girl. Before she could express her astonishment, he rode away.

Walter returned from the forest to find Elsa weeping. The golden garland lay broken at her feet. She flung her arms around his neck.

"Ah, Walter, I feared you were killed! After the golden knight rode away, a band of robber knights took advantage of the tournament to attack the king. Many loyal knights have been slain. The three princesses have been carried off. No one is left to pursue."

"There is one," said Walter. He ran to the forest. Iron John met him at the spring with a fiery war horse, a sword, and a gilded suit of battle armor.

"I know what you require," the wild man said.

"Thank you, Iron John, my truest friend," Walter replied. Armored head to foot, with sword in hand, he galloped off in pursuit of the robbers.

The golden knight caught the traitors at the edge of the forest. He slew some; the rest fled. The princesses were free. But before they could thank their redeemer, he rode away, blood dripping from his saddle. The golden knight had been wounded.

For days afterward the three princesses awaited news of their champion. No one noticed or cared that Walter-in-the-Mud was also missing. Only Elsa did. She grieved alone and out of sight.

Just when the princesses had given up hope, they beheld a strange procession approaching the castle. A king with an iron crown led a parade of men-at-arms who carried a litter upon which a dying knight lay. A veil covered the young knight's face.

"Who are you? What knight is this?" the princesses asked the king.

He answered, "My name is Iron John. An ancient curse changed me into a wild man. The spell is broken and I am free. But it has cost me one I hold dearer than my life. He is called the golden knight. He is wounded unto death. Only the tears of a maid who loves him truly can heal him."

Tears of joy and sorrow mingled in the eyes of the princesses. Their champion still lived. Surely they could save him. They gathered around the litter as the king removed the veil from the golden knight's face.

"It is Walter-in-the-Mud!" they cried. Their tears dried as fast as summer rains. Each one looked to her sisters to weep over Walter's grimy face, but none would do it. They couldn't. He was too dirty.

Then Elsa the garden girl pushed her way between them. "Dear Walter!" she cried as she cradled his head against her heart. Her tears fell upon his face, washing the mud away.

Walter opened his eyes. He threw back the coverlet and stepped from the litter, Walter-in-the-Mud no more, but a shining prince with hair of purest gold. He lifted Elsa in his arms. "This is my bride," he told the astonished princesses. "In Iron John's kingdom, she will be my queen." Then he mounted his horse and together with Elsa followed Iron John to his lands far away.

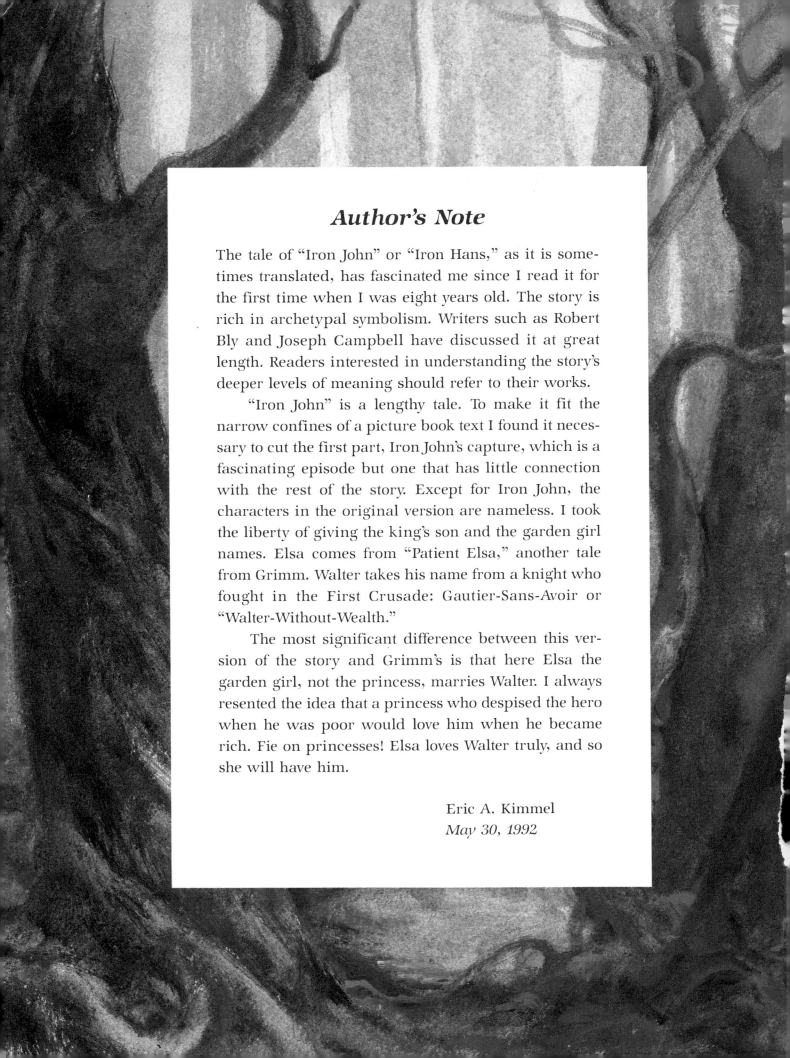

Author's Note

The tale of "Iron John" or "Iron Hans," as it is some-
times translated, has fascinated me since I read it for
the first time when I was eight years old. The story is
rich in archetypal symbolism. Writers such as Robert
Bly and Joseph Campbell have discussed it at great
length. Readers interested in understanding the story's
deeper levels of meaning should refer to their works.

"Iron John" is a lengthy tale. To make it fit the
narrow confines of a picture book text I found it neces-
sary to cut the first part, Iron John's capture, which is a
fascinating episode but one that has little connection
with the rest of the story. Except for Iron John, the
characters in the original version are nameless. I took
the liberty of giving the king's son and the garden girl
names. Elsa comes from "Patient Elsa," another tale
from Grimm. Walter takes his name from a knight who
fought in the First Crusade: Gautier-Sans-Avoir or
"Walter-Without-Wealth."

The most significant difference between this version of the story and Grimm's is that here Elsa the
garden girl, not the princess, marries Walter. I always
resented the idea that a princess who despised the hero
when he was poor would love him when he became
rich. Fie on princesses! Elsa loves Walter truly, and so
she will have him.

Eric A. Kimmel
May 30, 1992